The Lion
and the Rat

A FABLE BY
LA FONTAINE

The
Lion and the Rat

Illustrated by

BRIAN WILDSMITH

OXFORD UNIVERSITY PRESS

One day, a rat

walked, by accident, between a lion's paws.

But the lion
allowed him to
escape, unharmed.

The rat thanked the lion, and said: 'One day
I shall repay you for your kindness.'

The lion laughed to himself.
'How could such a tiny creature
help me, the Lord of the Jungle?'
he thought.

A few months later, the lion was out hunting in the forest when he fell into a trap.

He roared
in fury, and
struggled
with all
his might.

but he could not escape.

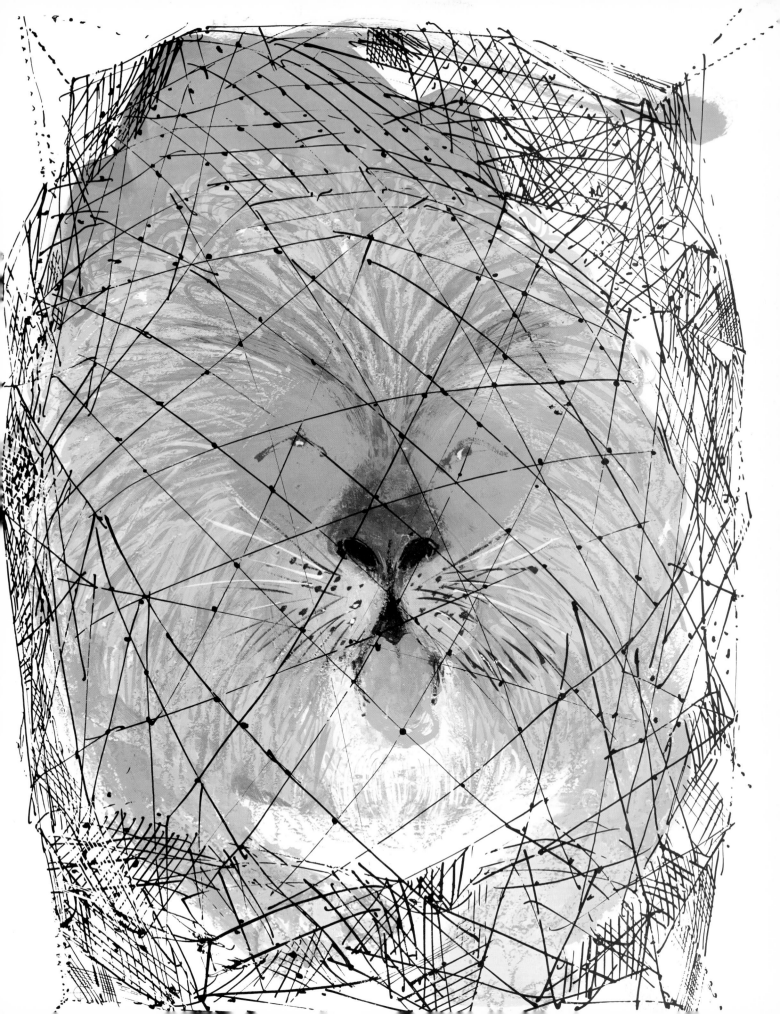

All the animals heard the lion,

and rushed to find him.

The lion asked each of them

in turn for help, but they said: 'How can weak
creatures like us help you, the Lord of the Jungle?'

And so they went away.

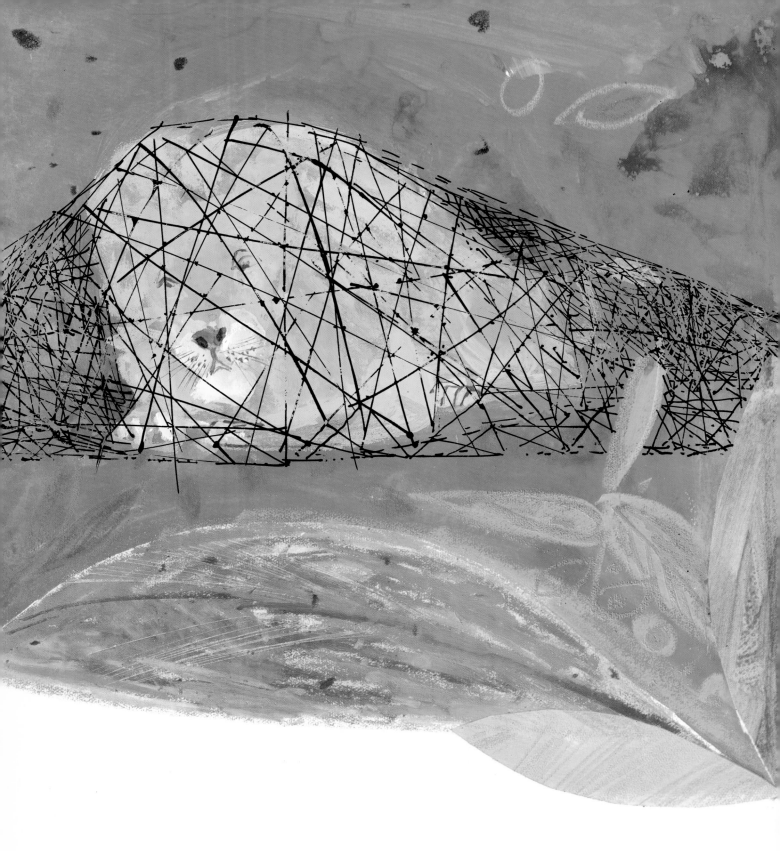

Just then, the rat came by.
He saw the lion in trouble and ran to help him.

He gnawed and gnawed
right through the net, until
at last the lion was freed.

So the little rat, by patience
and hard work, was able to
do what the lion, in all his
strength and rage, could not.

Oxford University Press, Walton Street, Oxford OX2 6DP

Oxford New York Toronto
Delhi Bombay Calcutta Madras Karachi
Petaling Jaya Singapore Hong Kong Tokyo
Nairobi Dar es Salaam Cape Town
Melbourne Auckland

and associated companies in
Berlin Ibadan

Oxford is a trade mark of Oxford University Press

ISBN 0 19 272167 4 (paperback)
ISBN 0 19 279607 0 (hardback)

© Brian Wildsmith 1963 First published 1963

Reprinted 1964, 1965, 1967, 1970, 1974, 1984 (twice), 1986, 1989
First published 1986 in paperback
Reprinted 1989

Printed in Hong Kong